Cinderella

Retold by Susanna Davidson

Illustrated by Lorena Alvarez

Not all stepmothers are wicked, but dear oh dear,
Cinderella's was very, very bad!

From morning till night, she made Cinderella cook and carry, clean and scrub. Cinderella even had to look after her horrible stepsisters.

Every day her stepmother would screech, "Hurry up you wretched girl! I want my lunch and I want it now!"

At night, Cinderella had to sleep on the floor
by the fire, among the cinders and ashes.

Then one morning an invitation arrived:
His Royal Highness, Prince Charming,
invites the ladies of the house to his Royal Ball.

"Of course Cinderella can't go," sneered her stepmother.
"She's just a servant."

On the night of the ball, Cinderella stood alone in the kitchen, tears sliding down her cheeks. "I want to go to the ball," she wept.

"And so you shall,"
said a musical voice.

"Don't be afraid. I am your fairy godmother."

"Really? Truly?" gasped Cinderella.

"You have my fairy promise," said her godmother.
"But first, I need a pumpkin."

Cinderella ran to the garden and picked
the biggest, plumpest pumpkin she could find.

The fairy tapped it with her wand.
The pumpkin rose up, growing bigger...
and rounder... then **BANG!**

"A golden coach to whisk you to the ball,"
smiled the fairy godmother.

Spell followed magical spell.
Six white mice became six proud horses,
tossing their silky manes.

A fat rat turned into a
whiskery coachman.

Six lizards were transformed into footmen,
dressed in glittering green.

Last of all came a ballgown, golden
yellow and laced with flowers.

"Thank you!" said Cinderella.
On her feet were a pair of glass
slippers, the prettiest she'd ever seen.

"Just remember," said her
godmother. "You must leave
before the clock strikes midnight.
For then my magic will
start to fade."

At the Royal Palace, Cinderella swept into a splendid ballroom...

"Will you dance with me?" asked the prince.

As they twirled and spun, a whisper followed them
around the room... "Who is that beautiful girl?"

"She must be a princess," moaned Cinderella's stepsister. "But I'm sure the prince would much rather dance with me."

Cinderella wished the dance could last forever. But all too soon, the clock struck midnight. "I must go!" she cried.

As she dashed down the palace steps, her dress turned back to rags. Her carriage was a pumpkin. Her coachman was a rat.

The prince ran after her. All that was left
was a glass slipper, sparkling on the steps.

Cinderella ran home, beneath the starry sky.
She kept her adventure a secret, and that night,
she slept with a smile on her lips.

The prince longed to find the mystery girl who had danced herself into his dreams.

He searched the land with the glass slipper, declaring, "I'll marry the girl who fits this shoe!"

At last, he came to Cinderella's house.
"It will fit me!" screeched her stepsisters, snatching
the shoe. They squeezed and squashed and squirmed...

...then screamed. No matter what they did,
they couldn't get the shoe to fit.

"May I try it on?" asked Cinderella,
coming quietly into the room.

"No!" snapped her stepmother. But it was too late.

Cinderella had put on the shoe... and it was a perfect fit.

The room sparkled with stars.
Cinderella's ragged clothes turned to gold.
She was dressed in her ballgown once more.
Her stepmother looked on aghast.

"At last!" cried the prince. "I've found you."

They were married the very next day.
Everyone was invited to the wedding,
the stepmother and her horrible
daughters, too.

Cinderella had such a kind heart she forgave her family,
and she and her prince lived happily ever after.

Cinderella is one of the most popular European fairy tales. There are many different versions around the world. This one is based on Charles Perrault's *Cinderella, or The Little Glass Slipper.* The oldest known version dates back to the sixth century B.C. and is about a Greek slave girl who marries the King of Egypt.

Edited by Lesley Sims
Designed by Samantha Barrett

First published in 2014 by Usborne Publishing Ltd., Usborne House, 83-85 Saffron Hill, London EC1N 8RT, England.
www.usborne.com   Copyright © 2014 Usborne Publishing Ltd.